W9-AZB-225

Dear Parents:

Congratulations! Your child is taking the first steps on an exciting journey. The destination? Independent reading!

STEP INTO READING® will help your child get there. The program offers five steps to reading success. Each step includes fun stories and colorful art or photographs. In addition to original fiction and books with favorite characters, there are Step into Reading Non-Fiction Readers, Phonics Readers and Boxed Sets, Sticker Readers, and Comic Readers—a complete literacy program with something to interest every child.

Learning to Read, Step by Step!

Ready to Read   Preschool–Kindergarten
• big type and easy words • rhyme and rhythm • picture clues
For children who know the alphabet and are eager to begin reading.

Reading with Help   Preschool–Grade 1
• basic vocabulary • short sentences • simple stories
For children who recognize familiar words and sound out new words with help.

Reading on Your Own   Grades 1–3
• engaging characters • easy-to-follow plots • popular topics
For children who are ready to read on their own.

Reading Paragraphs   Grades 2–3
• challenging vocabulary • short paragraphs • exciting stories
For newly independent readers who read simple sentences with confidence.

Ready for Chapters   Grades 2–4
• chapters • longer paragraphs • full-color art
For children who want to take the plunge into chapter books but still like colorful pictures.

STEP INTO READING® is designed to give every child a successful reading experience. The grade levels are only guides; children will progress through the steps at their own speed, developing confidence in their reading.

Remember, a lifetime love of reading starts with a single step!

Published in the United States by Random House Children's Books, a division of Penguin Random House LLC, 1745 Broadway, New York, NY 10019, and in Canada by Penguin Random House Canada Limited, Toronto.

Step into Reading, Random House, and the Random House colophon are registered trademarks of Penguin Random House LLC.

Visit us on the Web!
StepIntoReading.com
rhcbooks.com

Educators and librarians, for a variety of teaching tools, visit us at RHTeachersLibrarians.com
ISBN 978-0-593-31001-4 (trade) — ISBN 978-0-593-31002-1 (lib. bdg.) — ISBN 978-0-593-31003-8 (ebook)
Printed in the United States of America
10 9 8 7 6 5 4 3 2
2020 Random House Children's Books Edition

LET'S BE FRIENDS

by B.B. Arthur

Random House New York

Meet the outrageous members of the L.O.L. Surprise! squad! Life is always fierce and fun when you start a club with your best friends.

©MGA

The Glitterati Club is full
of sparkly queens.
Queen Bee *bee*-lieves in herself.
She is swanky in black and gold.

Kitty Queen always lands
on her feet.

Her kitty ears are the *purr*-fect
accessory.

Sugar Queen is super sassy
and super sweet.
She adores glitter and always lives
the sweet life.

Boss Queen runs the world.
She is in charge
and always makes
it work.

Art is life for the Art Club.

Pop Heart draws bold lines.

She totally lives life in primary colors.

Splatters paints outside the lines.

She might make a mess,

but it will always be a work of art.

EXPRESS URSELF

Every day is a costume party

in the Cosplay Club.

Bon Bon rocks pastel punk.

She thinks it is pretty sweet.

©MGA

Neon QT always stands out.

She knows brighter is better.

When it comes to color,

she wants it all!

Glam Club does it up right.

But not all princesses

wear glass slippers.

Miss Punk was born to stand out

with edgy style.

Whatever As If Baby wants,

As If Baby gets.

She is totally a laugh and a half.

The Glee Club loves to sing.

Diva slays.

Rocker rocks.

MC Swag never drops the hot tunes.

In Opposites Club,

differences shine.

Fresh brings the chill.

Fancy brings the frill.

Fresh's style is street.

Fancy's style is sweet.

Yin and Yang
balance the scales.
When they are together,
they make perfect
harmony.

In Theater Club,

being a drama queen

is a good thing.

Merbaby is on her own wave.

She lives for the stage

©MGA

Only pop idols join the Pop Club.

Daring Diva is playing your song.

80s BB strikes a pose.

Oops Baby is lost in the game.

©MGA

The Hip Hop Club
spins fresh beats.
DJ makes
the most amazing mixes.

Rock Club rocks out.
Punk Boi makes music
and mischief.

In Retro Club,

everything old is new.

Soul Babe is far out.

Go-Go Gurl is groovy.

HI!!

HI BAE!

26

STEM Club loves science.

VRQT is a super-smart tech guru.

She and PhD B.B. are always

on the cutting edge.

Sleepover Club

never forgets their pillows.

Snuggle Babe is a night owl

who dreams in black-and-white.

In Storybook Club,
stories come alive.
Bhaddie wants to hear the one
about the witch and her wicked ways.

In their totally cute clubs,
each fierce friend
does what she loves.
That is how they really shine . . .

. . . and sparkle!

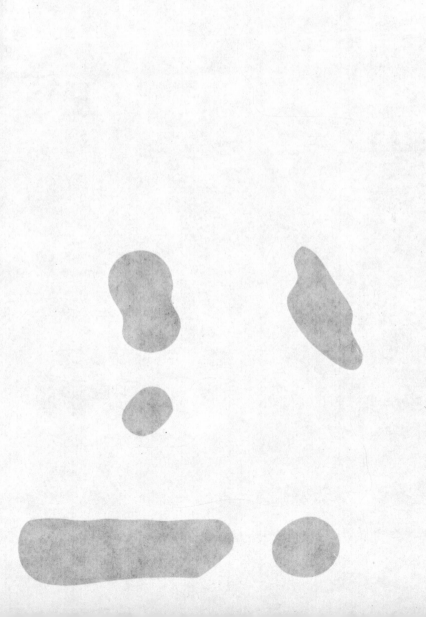

GLAM LIFE
©MGA

EXPRESS URSELF
©MGA

©MGA

©MGA

©MGA

#SQUADGOALS
©MGA

©MGA

©MGA

©MGA

©MGA

©MGA

©MGA

©MGA

Cute But Fierce
©MGA

©MGA

#SQUADGOALS

GLAM

HELLO!

BFFS 4EVA

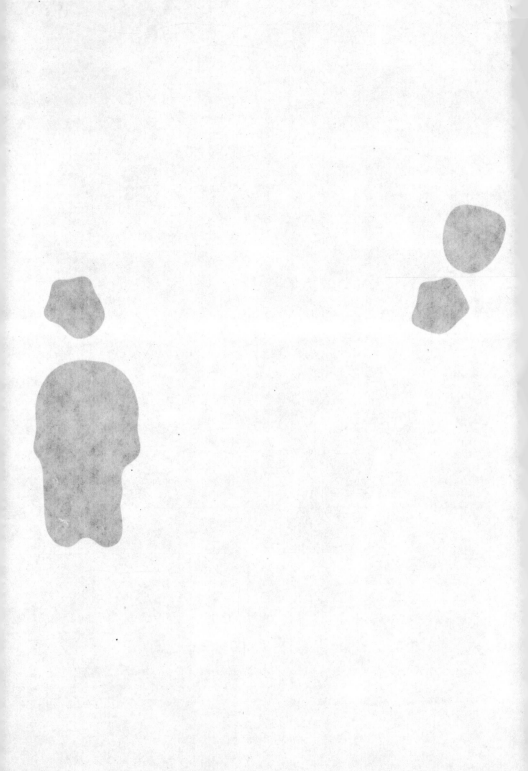